SERIOUSLY SILLY

SCARY
FAIRY TALES

SNOW FRIGHT
and the SEVEN
SKELETONS

ORCHARD BOOKS
338 Euston Road, London NW1 3BH
Orchard Books Australia
Level 17/207 Kent Street, Sydney, NSW 2000

First published in 2014 by Orchard Books

ISBN 978 1 40832 962 7

A CIP catalogue record for this book is available
from the British Library.

3 5 7 9 10 8 6 4 2
Printed in Great Britain

Orchard Books is a division of Hachette Children's Books,
an Hachette UK company.

www.hachette.co.uk

SERIOUSLY SILLY

SCARY
FAIRY TALES

SNOW FRIGHT
and the SEVEN
SKELETONS

Laurence Anholt
& Arthur Robins

ORCHARD

www.anholt.co.uk

GOOD EVENING, LADIES AND GENTLEMEN.

My name is

THE MAN WITHOUT A HEAD.

Of course I have a head really... It's just that my head is removable. I take it off at night and keep it safely in my bedside drawer.

So, you like SCARY STORIES, do you?

Well, I warn you, the stories I am about to tell are so TERRIFYING that grown men have been known to do wee wees in their panties.

If you are one of those people who believes that skeletons are bone-idle, I have a bone to pick with you - this is a story about seven very hard working skeletons.

Have you ever been to a funfair? I expect you laughed on the dodgem cars and stuffed your little face with toffee apples?

Perhaps you won a goldfish to take home with you?

I'd like to tell you about a girl named Snow Fright who worked at a very different kind of funfair – perhaps we should call it a FEAR FAIR!

Snow Fright's father owned a ghost train and he was very proud of it. He thought that his train was the most terrifying train ride in the world. Some people said that he paid real ghosts and skeletons to work inside. Snow Fright's father called his ride:

THE ROLLER GHOSTER

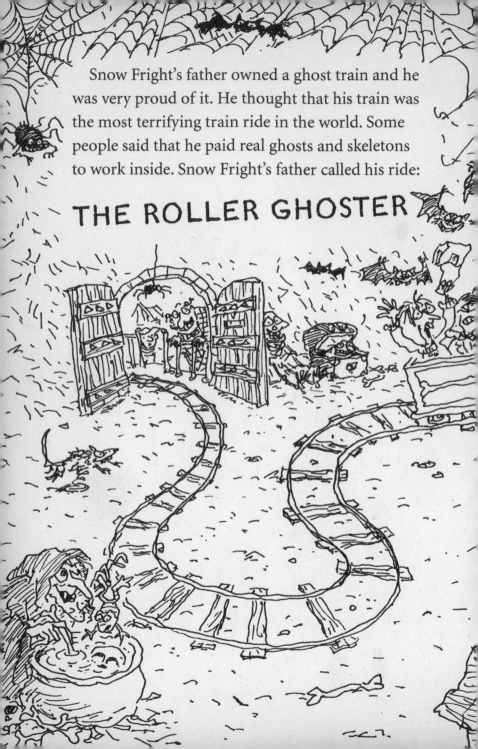

Snow Fright loved to be scared. Even when she was tiny, she would beg her father for a ride on the Roller Ghoster. She laughed as the little train rolled slowly through the creaky doors.

She squealed as it disappeared into the dark tunnel and clattered along the tracks.

She put her hands over her eyes when she heard the screams and groans inside.

And when the little trains came crashing out
at the other end, her hair was standing on end
and her face was so pale that everyone called her
Snow Fright.

Everyone at the funfair loved Snow Fright – they often gave her a free ride or let her win a little prize. But the person who loved Snow Fright more than anyone in the world was Ginger McCoy, the candyfloss boy. Every day, Ginger would give Snow Fright a huge pink candyfloss on a stick.

Yes, everyone loved Snow Fright...except one person! Next door to the Roller Ghoster was the Hall of Magic Mirrors. Here people could see themselves change shape before their eyes.

Fat people became thin; thin people became fat; tiny people became tall and tall people became tiny.

The Hall of Magic Mirrors was the most popular attraction at the fun fair. It was owned by Queenie O'Grady, the amazing Bearded Lady, the hairiest woman in the land.

Queenie O'Grady hated Snow Fright. She would stand in front of her strange mirrors and say –

Magic mirrors at the fair,
Who has got the weirdest hair?

Then the mirrors would reply –

You, oh Queen, are the Bearded Lady
None has more hair than
Queenie O'Grady.

Then Queenie O'Grady would laugh and laugh and go and get another tattoo on her back.

Ah, haar, haar haaa-aaar!

As Snow Fright grew older, her hair grew longer too. The more she rode on the Roller Ghoster, the more it stood on end. Ginger McCoy thought she had grown into the most beautiful girl in the world.

As the years passed, Queenie O'Grady began to notice that fewer people were coming to look at her beard or her Magic Mirrors. And the queues outside the Roller Ghoster were longer and longer.

Queenie would have loved to ride on the Roller Ghoster too, but secretly, she was terrified of spooks and skeletons. How she hated Snow Fright and her pale face and tall, long black hair.

One terrible day, Queenie O'Grady stood before her many magical mirrors and said –

Magic mirrors on the wall
Who has the weirdest hair of all?

To her horror, the mirrors replied –

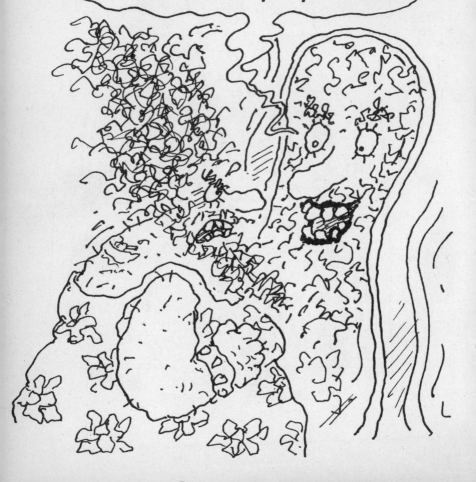

Queenie O'Grady turned green and yellow with jealousy and stormed outside. There was Snow Fright selling tickets in her father's little booth. Queenie couldn't believe her eyes – there was a queue a mile long! Not only was the Roller Ghoster the scariest ride in the funfair, but everyone was flocking to see Snow Fright. Now her hair had grown so tall that her father had built an extra tower on the roof of the ticket booth.

That day, the queue for the Roller Ghoster was so long that Snow Fright had to sit late into the evening selling tickets.

"You go to bed, Father," she said kindly. "I will stay here until the last customer has gone. Then I will lock up the ghost train and go to bed too."

Queenie couldn't think about anything except Snow Fright and the queue of customers admiring her hair. She began to make a terrible plan…

Late into the night, Snow Fright sold tickets. The moon came up and finally, the last customer had gone. Snow Fright swept up the ticket booth, then she went to lock the Roller Ghoster.

Just as she was turning the key, a hairy figure came out of the shadows, pushed Snow Fright into a train, and locked the door of the Roller Ghoster. Alas! It was Queenie O'Grady, the Bearded Lady –

Guess where you're going to spend the night?
With the SKELETONS, Snow Fright!
AH, HAAR, HAAR HAAA-AAAR!

Then Queenie O'Grady slipped the Roller Ghoster key in her pocket and crept silently back to the Hall of Magic Mirrors.

Inside the Roller Ghoster, Snow Fright's train rolled slowly along the dark track. She heard strange moans and groans. Chains rattled and bats flittered through the dark trees. To her horror, she realised that hundreds of cobwebs were clinging to her beautiful hair.

Snow Fright rolled on and on. At last, tired and afraid, her little train stopped beneath a signpost. Snow Fright climbed out and read the words:

HAUNTED COTTAGE THIS WAY

Around the corner was the creepiest little house she had ever seen. Exhausted and hungry, she rang the bell. But there was no one home. After a while, she sat on a bench outside.

While she was resting, seven skeletons who worked in the Roller Ghoster were returning from a hard day frightening children. As they walked, they sang a little song:

Hi ho, hi ho!

It's home from work we go

We spend all day

Scaring folk away

Hi ho, hi ho!

"Oh, I'm
dead tired," said
the first skeleton.

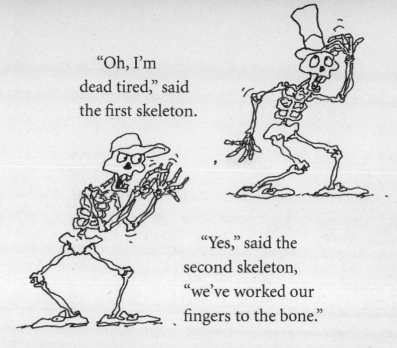

"Yes," said the
second skeleton,
"we've worked our
fingers to the bone."

"Help!" shouted the smallest skeleton, pointing
at Snow Fright. "There's something strange outside
our house."

"Don't be frightened," said Snow Fright. "What sweet little skeletons you are. Tell me, what are your names?"

"I'm Bony."

"I'm Tony."

"I'm Baloney."

"I'm Skelly."

"I'm Kelly."

"And I'm Shelly."

"And what about you?" said Snow Fright, pointing to the smallest skeleton.

"Oh, that's Baby Bonaparte," laughed all the other skeletons.

"Well, I am very happy to meet you," said Snow Fright. "Now please tell me how I can get out of the Roller Ghoster."

"No one can get out of the Roller Ghoster at night," said Bony.

"Except Bonaparte, of course," said Baloney.

"Every night he goes off to get our supper," said Kelly.

"He crawls through the letter box," said Skelly.

"But what do skeletons eat?" asked Snow Fright.

shouted all the
skeletons together.

So, Snow Fright held Baby Bonaparte's bony little hand and they walked back through the Roller Ghoster to the little door. Then Baby Bonaparte squeezed out through the letter box.

"Please find Queenie O'Grady and ask her for the key," called Snow Fright.

At that moment, Queenie O'Grady was standing in front of her Magic Mirrors.

Snow Fright is pretty as a poster
But she'll spend the night in the
ROLLER GHOSTER…

AH, HAAR, HAAR HAAA-AAAR!

Just then, Queenie O'Grady saw Baby Bonaparte
walking up behind her. In the magic mirror, he
looked like the biggest skeleton in the world.
Queenie O'Grady SCREAMED –

AAAA-AAAAR GH!!

Until her beard and all her hair stood on end.

Then Baby Bonaparte took the keys and went to visit Ginger McCoy, the Candyfloss Boy.

"Eight pink ones, please Ginger," he said.

"Hello, Baby Bonaparte," said Ginger McCoy. "Why do you want eight pink ones? There are only seven skeletons at the haunted cottage."

"We have a guest tonight," said Baby Bonaparte. "Snow Fright is locked inside the Roller Ghoster."

So, Ginger McCoy pushed his candyfloss machine across the fair to the Roller Ghoster. Baby Bonaparte unlocked the door and Ginger pushed his candyfloss machine along the railway track to the haunted cottage, where Snow Fright was sitting on the bench with the small skeletons.

Snow Fright was very pleased to see Ginger McCoy and Ginger McCoy was very pleased to see Snow Fright. For a special treat, he made red, white and blue candyfloss.

"Oh, you are clever," gasped Snow Fright.

When they were finished, Snow Fright and Ginger held hands and pushed the candyfloss machine back along the railway track. Far away in the dark shadows of the Roller Ghoster, they could hear a beautiful song:

Hi ho, hi ho!
It's off to bed we go
We said good night
To our friend Snow Fright
Hi ho, hi ho!

And that was the terrifying story of Snow Fright and the Seven Skeletons. Make no bones about it – every word was true. I hope it tickled your funny bone.

Oh yes, I forgot to mention, when Snow Fright's father grew too old to run the Roller Ghoster, Snow Fright and Ginger McCoy set up business together. Next time you go to the fair, you may take a ride on the Roller Ghoster, while you tuck into Ginger's red, white and blue candyfloss.

Then, if you are very brave, you might go next door to the Hall of Magic Mirrors, and meet Queenie O'Grady, the hair-raising Bearded Lady.

SERIOUSLY SILLY

SCARY
FAIRY TALES

LAURENCE ANHOLT & ARTHUR ROBINS

COLLECT THEM ALL!

Also available as an ebook